POKéMON

THE JOHTO JOURNEYS

Winner Takes All

Pokémon World

Words and Music by John Loeffler (ASCAP)/John Siegler (BMI)

Rap:

So you wanna be a master of
POKéMON
Understand the Secrets and
HAVE SOME FUN
So you wanna be a master of Pokémon
POKéMON
Do you have the skills to be
NUMBER ONE?

Verse I:

I wanna take the ultimate step
Find the courage to be bold
To risk it all and not forget
The lessons that I hold

I wanna go where no one's been
Far beyond the crowd
Learn the way to take command
Use the power that's in my hand

Chorus:

We all live in a Pokémon World
I want to be the greatest master of them all
We all live in a Pokémon World
Put myself to the test
Be better than all the rest

Verse II:

Every day along the way
I will be prepared
With every challenge I will gain
Knowledge to be shared

In my heart there's no doubt
Of who I want to be
Right here standing strong
The greatest Master of Pokémon

Chorus

Rap: You've got the power right in your hands

There are more books about Pokémon.

Collect them all!

POKÉMON

THE JOHTO JOURNEYS

Winner Takes All

Adapted by Tracey West

SCHOLASTIC INC.
New York   Toronto   London   Auckland   Sydney
Mexico City   New Delhi   Hong Kong   Buenos Aires

JOHTO REGION

ISBN 0-439-35802-7

© 2001 Pokemon.
© 1995 — 2001 Nintendo/Creatures Inc./GAME FREAK Inc. TM and ® are trademarks of Nintendo.
All rights reserved. Published by Scholastic Inc.
SCHOLASTIC and associated logos are trademarks and/or registered trademarks of Scholastic Inc.

12 11 10 9 8 7   7/0

Printed in the U.S.A.
First Scholastic printing, April 2002

Winner Takes All

1

Battle at the Goldenrod Gym

"Look out, Cyndaquil!" Ash Ketchum yelled.

Beads of sweat rolled down Ash's face as he watched his Pokémon on the battlefield. He was in the middle of a battle against Whitney — leader of the Goldenrod Gym — and her team of Pokémon.

Ash had started by calling out Cyndaquil, a feisty Fire Pokémon. The small Pokémon looked cute, but powerful flames came out of its back when it attacked.

Ash was confident Cyndaquil could take

on anything Whitney dished out. But he didn't know what to expect when Whitney called on Miltank.

The milk cow Pokémon had a light pink body with four udders dotting its white belly. Its ears were black, and black spots marked its back. Its face seemed friendly.

But Miltank's attacks were anything but friendly.

"Miltank, Rollout!" Whitney cried.

Miltank curled into a ball and rolled toward Cyndaquil at lightning speed. The Pokémon looked like a blur, it was moving so fast.

"Cyndaquil!" Ash cried again, but his Pokémon couldn't move in time.

Wham! Miltank slammed into the other Pokémon like a bowling ball knocking down a pin. Cyndaquil went flying.

Ash called on his next Pokémon, Totodile. The Water Pokémon had sharp teeth and a powerful Water Gun Attack.

Whitney called on Miltank before Ash could make a move.

"Miltank, Rollout!" she cried.

Ash groaned as Miltank rolled toward Totodile. The attack was practically unstoppable.

"Get out of its way, Totodile!" Ash yelled.

Once again, Miltank was too fast and agile.

Wham! Totodile went flying.

Ash gritted his teeth. He could only use three Pokémon in this battle. He had already used two — he'd need to use his best Pokémon to stay in the game.

"Pikachu, I choose you!" Ash cried.

The little Electric Pokémon was Ash's first Pokémon and now his trusted friend. Pikachu jumped into the battle arena.

Miltank rolled toward Pikachu. Pikachu's small yellow body sizzled with energy as it hurled an electric blast at Miltank.

"Yes!" Ash cheered.

But Miltank was rolling so fast, the electricity bounced right off its pink body.

Pikachu wasn't expecting that. It had no time to react.

Slam! Pikachu went down, just like Ash's other Pokémon.

"Sorry, Ash," Whitney said. "I guess your Pokémon are no match for my Miltank."

Whitney's words stung, but there was no time to dwell on them. Ash took his injured Pokémon to the Pokémon Center in town. There, Nurse Joy would care for them until they recovered from the battle.

Ash sulked in the waiting room while Nurse Joy attended to Cyndaquil, Totodile, and Pikachu. His friends Misty and Brock tried to comfort him.

"You did your best, Ash," Misty said. "That Miltank's Rollout was too powerful."

"The more times it collides, the more powerful its attack becomes," Brock said. "That's hard to beat."

Ash knew his friends were right but it didn't make him feel any better.

Ash was training to be a Pokémon Master. To achieve that goal, he would have to travel around the world catching and training new Pokémon. He also had to challenge gym leaders to battles so he could gain experience and earn gym badges. He had traveled a long way to fight Whitney at the Goldenrod Gym — for nothing.

"There has to be some way to beat Miltank," Ash said. "And I won't rest until I figure it out!"

2

The Miltank Ranch

Ash spent a restless night at the Pokémon Center. Moonlight streamed through the window of the lobby, lighting up Misty's orange hair as she slept soundly in her sleeping bag. Togepi, Misty's tiny spike ball Pokémon, was curled up beside her. Brock was sound asleep, too. But Ash just couldn't seem to get any rest. His mind raced with thoughts of the battle and his injured Pokémon.

Ash finally drifted off to sleep and woke up a few hours later as sunlight filled the

Pokémon Center. Chansey walked into the lobby. Cyndaquil, Totodile, and Pikachu stood beside it. They all looked as good as new.

"You're all right!" Ash cried. He ran over and hugged each one.

Just then, Whitney walked into the Pokémon Center. Her pink ponytails bobbed as she walked. She wore a white shirt and white shorts with red trim.

"Everyone looks better. That's great!" she said cheerfully. Then she scooped up

Pikachu. "Come on, I'm going to take you all to a really great place."

There was no arguing with Whitney's forceful personality. They followed her out of the Pokémon Center. Whitney chatted about her Miltank as they walked across town. Soon they came to a big green field surrounded by a wooden fence. Pink Miltank dotted the field. Most were sleeping in the grass. Ash saw Whitney's Miltank in the field, too.

"It's a Miltank ranch. A friend of mine runs it," she said.

Ash spotted a figure walking toward them. The man looked like a cowboy. He wore a red scarf around his neck and a brown vest. His gray mustache matched the hair on his head.

"Hey, Milton!" Whitney called out.

"Whitney, is that you?" the man replied.

Whitney introduced them all to Milton. Ash liked the man from the start. Milton took them all to the ranch house and poured them each a glass of cold milk.

"Wow, this is delicious," Ash said as he downed his glass.

"It's Miltank milk," said Milton proudly, "the best milk in the Johto Region."

The room got quiet as the others finished their milk. Pikachu and Togepi happily lapped up theirs from a bowl.

Then a loud crash interrupted them.

"What was that?" Ash wondered.

"It came from the kitchen," Whitney said. She quickly ran out of the room.

Ash heard Whitney cry out. Then three figures burst from the kitchen. There was a girl with long red hair, a boy with purple hair, and a short white scratch cat Pokémon.

Their arms were loaded with cheese and cartons of milk, but Ash still recognized them. They were Jessie, James, and Meowth.

"Team Rocket!" Ash cried. The terrible trio usually tried to steal Pokémon. Now it looked like they were stealing food.

Ash jumped up from his chair. "Pikachu, Thundershock!" he yelled.

They all ran out of the kitchen after Team Rocket. Pikachu led the way. As soon as there was a clear shot, Pikachu blasted Team Rocket with an electric surge.

Zap! Jessie, James, and Meowth sizzled with the charge. The food went flying out of their hands. Brock, Misty, and Milton caught it all as it fell.

Jessie spun around and scowled at Ash. "This calls for a Pokémon battle!" she shrieked.

Jessie threw a Poké Ball and Arbok, a purple Cobra Pokémon, flew out.

James threw a Poké Ball. Out came

Weezing, a Poison Pokémon that looked like a purple cloud with two heads.

Whitney stepped up next to Ash.

"If you want a battle, you'll get one," she said. "You're up, Miltank!"

Miltank ran to Whitney's side.

"Miltank, Rollout!" Whitney yelled.

Miltank rolled into a ball and sped toward Arbok and Weezing. Team Rocket's Pokémon didn't stand a chance. Miltank slammed into them. The Pokémon went flying back and crashed into Jessie, James, and Meowth.

Wham! Miltank slammed the entire group again. Team Rocket and their Pokémon sailed off into the sky.

"Looks like we're blasting off again!" they yelled.

"Great work, Miltank," Whitney said.

Ash turned to Whitney. "Your Miltank is great. I'd love to learn more about it."

Whitney nodded. "No problem. Miltank and I were about to do some training. Why don't you come watch?"

Ash and the others followed Whitney to a steep green hill. Miltank walked to the top.

"Go, Miltank!" Whitney cried.

Miltank curled into a ball and began rolling down the hill. When it neared the bottom, Whitney cried out again, "Now change direction!"

Miltank curved around and started rolling back up the hill.

"So that is the secret behind Miltank's power," Brock said. The older boy was interested in learning all he could about Pokémon. "Rolling uphill increases its strength."

Ash sighed. "I'll never be able to stand up to an attack like that," he said.

Suddenly, the ground beneath their feet began to shake. A thundering sound filled the air.

"What's happening?" Misty shouted over the noise.

"Something's coming," Ash shouted back. "And it can't be good!"

3

Team Rocket Strikes Back

Ash gasped as a huge wooden robot appeared at the top of the hill. It was shaped like a barrel.

Three figures popped out of the top of the giant barrel.

"Team Rocket!" Ash, Brock, and Misty cried at once.

Jessie grinned. "We'll help ourselves to this Miltank and your Pikachu," she said.

"It'll be a snap!" added Meowth.

Meowth pressed some buttons on a con-

trol panel it was holding. A metal arm with a big red hand came out of one end of the barrel.

The arm reached out and quickly grabbed Miltank.

"No!" Whitney cried.

Team Rocket disappeared inside the barrel. An angry Pikachu charged toward the robot.

A second metal arm extended from the other end of the barrel. Quick as a flash, it snatched up Pikachu.

"Pikachu!" Ash cried. He ran up the hill toward the robot.

The robot started to roll back down the other side of the hill. Sparks electrified the air as Pikachu tried to shock the robot, but the red hand kept absorbing the charge.

Meowth popped out of the robot. "Those robot hands are Pikachu-protected!" it jeered.

Ash knew he had to find a way to stop the barrel robot. He ran down the hill, tossing a Poké Ball into the air.

"Cyndaquil, I choose you!" Ash cried. The

Fire Pokémon appeared in a flash of light.
"Tackle its left side!"

Bright red flames burst from Cyndaquil's
back as it energized for the attack. The little
Pokémon ran up and slammed into the side
of the robot, shaking it.

Meanwhile, Ash threw another Poké Ball.
Totodile came flying out.

18

"Totodile, dig a hole in the ground with Water Gun!" Ash commanded.

Totodile aimed a powerful stream of water at the ground in front of the barrel. The water cut a deep trench into the dirt.

Ash watched as the robot barrel rolled toward the trench. The robot lost its balance and went careening in another direction.

"Keep it up, Totodile!" Ash yelled.

Whoosh! Whoosh! Whoosh! Totodile kept pumping streams of water into the dirt. More trenches appeared in the ground. Every time the robot hit one, it went flying in another direction.

The robot began to rattle and make creaking noises. Pieces of metal and wood started to fly off the barrel.

Ash heard James yell inside the machine. "The controls are broken! Now *we're* out of control!"

The two red robot hands released their grip. Miltank and Pikachu tumbled safely to the ground.

Jessie, James, and Meowth peered out of the robot.

"This is looking . . ." said Meowth.

". . . like another one of our . . ." said James.

". . . blastoffs!" finished Jessie.

As Team Rocket wailed, Pikachu jumped high in the air. It aimed an electrified thunderbolt right into the heart of the robot.

Blam! The robot exploded, and Team Rocket flew off into the distance.

Milton approached Ash. "You saved my ranch," he said. "Thank you."

Whitney hugged Miltank. "I owe you my thanks, too. What can I do to repay you?

Ash smiled. "Would you let me battle your Miltank again?" he asked.

"Here? Now?" Whitney asked.

Ash nodded. "That's right. I think I know how to beat Miltank now!"

4

Ash's Winning Strategy

"I accept your challenge, Ash," Whitney said.

"Great," Ash said. "If I win, how about you let me challenge you for a badge once more?"

Whitney nodded. "It's a deal."

Ash, Whitney, and their Pokémon walked to a flat part of the field where they could battle. Misty, Brock, and Milton stood on the sidelines.

"What is Ash thinking?" Misty wondered.

"He must have some kind of strategy," Brock remarked.

Whitney lunged right into the battle. "Miltank, Rollout!" she yelled.

Ash called on Cyndaquil. "Use Tackle!"

As Miltank rolled toward Cyndaquil, the Fire Pokémon leaped up and slammed into Miltank head-on. The impact sent Miltank veering in another direction, but it didn't stop rolling.

"Miltank, use full power!" Whitney yelled.

Miltank increased speed. This time, it hit

Cyndaquil before the Pokémon could fight back. Cyndaquil went flying, but it landed on its feet.

"Don't give in, Cyndaquil!" Ash cried.

Cyndaquil and Miltank volleyed back and forth. *Bam!* Cyndaquil tackled Miltank. *Bam!* Miltank rolled into Cyndaquil. The attacks were fast and furious, but finally Cyndaquil was too exhausted to continue.

"Good work, Cyndaquil," Ash said. "Totodile, you're next!"

Ash could see concern on Misty's face as she watched from the sidelines.

"What is Ash doing?" Misty asked Brock. "He's making the same mistakes as last time."

"Maybe it's part of his plan," Brock said. "Cyndaquil put up a good fight. Miltank must be getting tired out."

"Totodile, use Water Gun!" Ash called out.

Powerful streams of water exploded from Totodile's mouth. Ash directed his Pokémon to blast trenches into the dirt, just like it had done when fighting Team Rocket's robot.

His strategy was working. Miltank rolled

toward Totodile, but every time it hit a trench it bounced up and changed direction.

"Miltank, stay on track!" Whitney yelled.

Finally, Miltank straightened out its path. It was seconds away from slamming into Totodile.

"Totodile, jump!" Ash cried.

Whitney's eyes widened in disbelief as Totodile jumped on top of Miltank. Its feet moved quickly as it tried to keep its balance.

Miltank shook off Totodile. The little Water Pokémon went flying across the field. Miltank began rolling after it again, and this time, made contact.

Wham! The blow was all it took to pull Totodile out of the contest.

Ash knew that Totodile had done its job. It was time to finish things — with Pikachu.

"Go, Pikachu!" Ash cried.

Pikachu ran into the field. Miltank rolled toward it. Then . . .

Bam! Miltank rolled into one of the trenches Totodile had blasted into the ground. The impact sent it rolling away from Pikachu.

So far, everything was working exactly as Ash had planned.

"Pikachu, Agility!" Ash yelled.

Miltank regained its balance and started to roll after Pikachu. But the yellow Pokémon quickly dodged the attack. It ducked into one of the trenches, moving so fast that Whitney and Miltank didn't know where it went.

Miltank rolled over the field, searching for Pikachu. Pikachu waited patiently until it

saw Miltank roll over the trench. Then Pikachu jumped up out of the ground.

"Pikachuuuuuuuuuuuu!" Ash's Pokémon hurled a sizzling Thunderbolt at Miltank.

Miltank's body glowed with yellow electricity. Then it fell to the ground in a heap.

"Miltank!" Whitney cried.

"That did it," said Milton. "The battle's over."

Misty shook her head in disbelief. "Ash actually won."

Brock had it all figured out. "He used Cyndaquil's Tackle to exhaust Miltank. The milk cow Pokémon was worn down even more by the holes Totodile dug. Then Ash ended the battle with Pikachu's Thunderbolt. It was a beautiful strategy, using all of his Pokémons' strengths."

Ash approached Whitney and her Pokémon. "Are you okay, Miltank?" he asked.

"Miltank will be fine after a little rest," Whitney said. Then she reached into her pocket and pulled out a small, square object. It was brown with a silver border.

"This is a Plain Badge," Whitney said. She handed the badge to Ash. "It's yours."

"But shouldn't I battle you in the gym first?" Ash asked.

"Miltank is Whitney's best Pokémon," said Milton. "Since you've beaten it, you've earned the badge. Am I right, Whitney?"

"You said it," the gym leader agreed.

Ash grinned. He held the badge in the air. "I won a Plain Badge!" he cried.

5

The Bug-Catching Contest

Ash felt great after winning the Plain Badge. It proved he hadn't come all the way to the Johto Region for nothing. He still had more badges to win, but now Ash felt ready for any challenge that might lie ahead.

"I think I'm on a winning streak," Ash told Brock and Misty as they continued their journey.

"I wouldn't call one win a streak," Misty teased him.

"You know what I mean," Ash said. "I just feel like I can't lose."

Brock pointed to the distance. "It looks like you might have a chance to win again," he said.

Ash shaded his eyes. Just over the next hill was a small stadium. Colorful tents were set up outside. People were walking around dressed like Bug Pokémon. And a banner reading BUG-CATCHING CONTEST waved in the breeze.

"Contest? Sounds good to me!" Ash said. He ran toward the tents.

Inside the registration tent, Ash found a contest official.

"This is a nature preserve for Bug Poké-mon," the man told Ash. "We hold a contest every year. The winner receives a valuable prize and gets to keep one of the Bug Poké-mon caught in the preserve."

"Sign me up!" Ash said eagerly.

Brock and Misty caught up with Ash outside the tent. Misty looked very uncomfortable.

"Ash, you know how I feel about Bug Pokémon," Misty said, shivering. "They give me the creeps."

"You don't have to catch any, Misty," Ash said. "Just sit back and watch me win first prize!"

Behind him, a girl's voice laughed. "Well, if it isn't Ash and the gang!"

Ash turned around. A girl his age stood behind him, smiling. She wore a black-and-yellow baseball outfit. A baseball cap was perched on top of her blue ponytails. Next to her was a Chikorita, a light green Grass Pokémon.

"Hey, I remember you," Ash said. "You're Casey!" Ash had battled Casey and her Chikorita early in his journeys. Casey was a baseball fanatic. She liked to train her Pokémon as though she were a baseball coach.

"Looks like you're entering the bug contest," Casey said. "So am I."

Pikachu approached Chikorita, happy to see an old friend. Togepi jumped out of Misty's arms and waddled toward Chikorita.

"Togepi," chirped the little Pokémon cheerfully.

"Your Chikorita's looking great," Ash remarked. The Pokémon had a sturdy body and walked on four short legs. A green leaf grew from the top of its head, and several green dots ringed its neck.

Casey smiled confidently. "It sure is. That's why we're going to win this thing!"

Soon it was time for the contest to begin. Misty and Brock headed to the stands. Ash and Pikachu headed onto the stage in the

middle of the round stadium. Casey and the other competing trainers were lined up there. Ash took his place in line as the announcer stepped to the microphone. The heavyset man wore a blue suit and a gray beard covered his chin.

"Here are the rules. All trainers can use only one Pokémon," he said. "Each trainer must use this special Park Ball to catch the Bug Pokémon."

The announcer handed each trainer a Park Ball. Most Poké Balls were red on one half and white on the other, but the Park Ball was blue and white with a green flower marking.

"You only get one Park Ball, so if you catch one Pokémon and then find one you like better, you must let the first Pokémon go," the announcer explained. "The judging committee will decide which of the captured Pokémon is most impressive."

Ash listened carefully. The rules were a little tricky, but it was a fair contest. He was ready.

"Let the Bug-Pokémon-Catching Contest begin!" the announcer boomed.

6

Stalking Scyther

The stadium crowd cheered as Ash and the other trainers left the stage and headed into the nature preserve. A large video screen was lowered onto the stage so that the spectators could watch the trainers during the contest.

The preserve was a lush green space dotted with bushes and tall trees. Ash knew he would have to keep a sharp eye out if he was going to catch any Bug Pokémon. Some Pokémon, like small green Caterpie, blended into the green grass. Others, like Pineco, hung from tree branches, but their dark, bumpy skin was hard to spot against the tree bark.

Suddenly, Pikachu's ears began to twitch. *"Pika!"* said Pikachu.

Ash listened, too. Then he heard it. A munching sound. A small brown Weedle was chomping on the leaves of a nearby bush.

Weedle had a long, segmented body and a round red nose. Ash knew it had a powerful Poison Sting.

But Ash was in luck. The Weedle hadn't noticed him yet.

"Pikachu, Thundershock!" Ash yelled.

Before Pikachu could act, sharp green leaves whizzed through the air, knocking down the Weedle. Casey and her Chikorita came charging through the trees.

"Nice Razor Leaf Attack," Casey told her Chikorita. Then Ash watched, stunned, as she threw her Park Ball at Weedle.

The ball opened up, and the air was filled with white light. Weedle disappeared, and the ball snapped shut.

"All right!" Casey cheered. "I'm one run up in this ball game!"

Ash stepped in front of Casey. "Hold on a minute. We found this one first," he said angrily.

Casey shrugged. "The fastest hand wins. Sorry, Ash."

Ash stormed away with Pikachu at his

heels. Now he *had* to win this contest. He couldn't stand losing to Casey.

Ash looked up into the stadium, hoping to get some encouragement from his friends. Instead, he saw Misty shrieking as a Spinarak fell onto her lap.

"Why did we have to come to a Bug Poké-mon preserve?" she wailed.

Ash sighed and moved on.

"I'm not worried about losing that Weedle," he told Pikachu. "It will take a better Pokémon than that to win the contest, anyway."

Ash and Pikachu walked around the preserve, but they didn't spot anything. Suddenly, a loud cry pierced the air.

"*Scyyyyyy!*"

Ash knew that sound.

"It's a Scyther!" he said excitedly. The combination Bug/Flying Pokémon was about as tough as Bug Pokémon could get, and they were almost as big as Ash. If he caught a Scyther, he'd be sure to win the contest.

Ash and Pikachu followed the noise to a clearing. Scyther was circling the air over a fallen Pokémon.

It was Casey's Chikorita! Casey stood off to the side, cheering on her Pokémon.

"Keep up the energy!" she yelled out.

But Ash thought her Chikorita looked drained. Scyther swooped down from the sky at the Grass Pokémon, its sharp claws extended.

Chikorita ducked, just missing Scyther's claws. Then several sharp Razor Leaves flew out of the top of Chikorita's head.

Scyther wailed and swatted the leaves one by one. The leaves swung back and struck Chikorita.

The Grass Pokémon staggered around the field.

"Be careful, Casey," Ash called out. "Your Chikorita's about to be knocked out."

"Don't tell me how to play my game," Casey shot back.

Scyther scooped up Chikorita in its claws.

Slam! Scyther pounded Chikorita into a nearby tree trunk. Chikorita slumped to the ground.

"Pika!" Pikachu was angry now. It hurled an electric blast at Scyther.

"Scyther!" hissed the Pokémon. Then it darted off through the trees.

Ash turned to Casey. "We'll take care of Scyther," he said. "You'd better take care of your Chikorita!"

Then Ash and Pikachu ran after the escaping Scyther.

"Let's hurry, Pikachu," Ash said. "If we catch that Scyther, we'll have this contest in the bag!"

7

Beedrill Attack!

"Pikachu!"

Pikachu spotted the Scyther walking ahead of them. Ash quickly grabbed Pikachu and darted behind a nearby bush.

"I don't want Scyther to see us," Ash whispered. "We need to launch a sneak attack."

The Scyther circled around and started walking toward their hiding place. Ash gripped the Park Ball, ready for anything.

Suddenly, the quiet clearing was filled with a loud buzzing noise. Scyther zoomed away at the sound of it.

Soon Ash understood why. Five black-and-yellow-striped Pokémon flew out of the bushes behind them.

"Whoa. Beedrill!" Ash cried.

Beedrill was one of the coolest Bug Pokémon around. The sharp stingers on the ends of its hind legs struck fear into the hearts of even the toughest Pokémon.

Scyther might be gone, but catching a Beedrill would be just as good.

"Go, Park Ball!" Ash yelled. He threw the blue-and-white ball at one of the Beedrill.

It was no use. The Beedrill kicked it away with its powerful front legs.

"I guess I need to weaken it first," Ash said. "Pikachu, Thunderbolt!"

Pikachu jumped up and hurled a sizzling Thunderbolt at the Beedrill. The Beedrill was moving fast, but Pikachu's attack was faster.

Zap! The Beedrill fell to the grass. Ash threw the Park Ball before the Beedrill had a chance to recover.

The ball opened up, and Beedrill vanished in a glare of white light. Then the ball snapped shut.

The Park Ball rocked and wiggled as the Beedrill tried to escape. Ash held his breath. Then it finally stopped.

Ash reached down and grabbed the ball. "We did it!" he cried. "We caught a Beedrill!"

Ash and Pikachu jumped up and gave each other a high five in the air. But when Ash's feet hit the ground, he felt the dirt give way beneath him.

"Whoa!" Ash cried as he and Pikachu tumbled into a hole.

They were both a little dusty but okay.

"Who would have done something like this?" Ash wondered.

A metal cage dropped into the hole, trapping Ash and Pikachu. Ash looked up.

The cage was attached to a Meowth-shaped balloon. And inside the balloon were Jessie, James, and Meowth.

"Team Rocket!" Ash exclaimed.

Meowth grinned. "Our bug-catching plan worked beautifully," it said.

"Pikaaaa!" Pikachu tried to shock Team Rocket, but the Electric Attack couldn't reach as high as the balloon. Ash felt his body sizzle with the charge.

"We've caught a nice big firefly," James joked.

"How pretty," added Jessie. "Bug catching is fun!"

Ash's mind raced as he tried to figure out a way to escape. He pulled on the bars of the cage, but they wouldn't budge.

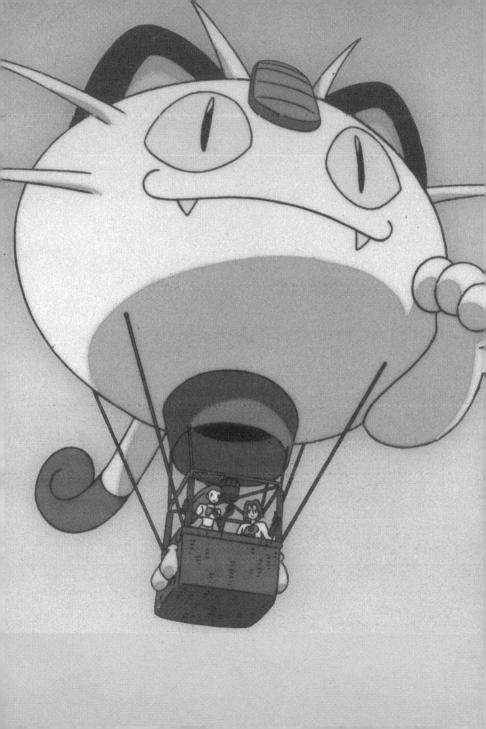

Meanwhile, the balloon was rising higher and higher into the air. Ash had to do something before Team Rocket got too far.

"Ash! Wait!" yelled a familiar voice.

Ash and Pikachu looked down. Misty and Brock had found them! Casey was there, too, with her Chikorita.

"Team Rocket, you're interfering with this game!" Casey called up to the balloon.

"Oh, it's that annoying girl who is batty for baseball," Jessie moaned.

Casey ignored Jessie's insult. She turned to her Chikorita.

"I'm sorry for pushing you too hard before," she told it. "Ash and Pikachu are our friends. Will you help me help them?"

Chikorita nodded.

"We won't even give you a chance to get up to bat," Meowth said. "This pitch will end the game!"

Meowth held up a remote-control device and pressed a button. A door in the bottom of the balloon opened up. A giant missile shaped like a baseball swooped down.

"A missile!" Misty shouted.

But Chikorita didn't back down. Its red eyes glowed with determination.

And that wasn't the only thing about Chikorita that was glowing. Ash watched in amazement as a golden light exploded from Chikorita's body.

"Chikorita is evolving!" Ash cried.

8

Bayleef to the Rescue

Before their eyes, Chikorita transformed into its evolved form. It had the same sturdy body, but its neck was much longer. Now there were green leaves instead of green dots growing from its neck.

"What's that?" Ash wondered. He took out Dexter, his Pokédex. The handheld computer contained information about all kinds of Pokémon.

"Bayleef, the Leaf Pokémon, is the evolved form of Chikorita," Dexter said. "Its Razor Leaf is extremely powerful. It can emit a spice scent from the leaves on its neck."

"This is great!" Casey said. "Just when we needed a pinch hitter. Go, Bayleef!"

"Launch the missile!" Jessie yelled from the balloon.

The baseball-shaped missile zoomed toward Bayleef. At Casey's command, a barrage of sharp Razor Leaves came flying from the top of Bayleef's head.

Zip! The leaves sliced through the missile. It fell to the ground like confetti.

Zip! More leaves sliced through the rope connecting the cage to the balloon basket. The cage opened and Ash and Pikachu tumbled safely to the ground.

"We did it! Home run!" Casey cheered.

Ash was getting into the spirit of Casey's baseball lingo. "Pikachu, put your all into this play, too," he said.

"Pika!" Sparks flew around Pikachu's body as it charged up for an Electric Attack.

"This is looking like bases loaded with no outs," James said, worried.

"Pikachuuuuuuu!" Pikachu hurled a jagged lightning bolt at the balloon. The balloon ex-

ploded, and Team Rocket went spiraling off into the sky.

"Game over!" they cried as they blasted off.

Ash started to thank Casey for her help when the announcer's voice blared throughout the nature preserve.

"The Bug-Catching Competition is over! All trainers please return to the judging area," he said.

"I hope this Beedrill is enough to win," Ash said.

Ash waited nervously as the judges examined all the Pokémon caught during the contest. He had to admit that his Beedrill looked good — but was it good enough to give him the win?

Finally, the judges announced a winner.

"Victory goes to Ash for capturing a Beedrill!" the announcer boomed. "As his reward, he'll receive a Sun Stone and can keep the Beedrill."

The announcer handed Ash his Park Ball, along with a glittering stone shaped like a sun.

"Congratulations, Ash," Casey said. "That was a really great game."

"I don't know who would have won if Team Rocket hadn't gotten in the way," Ash said.

Casey smiled. "That's okay," she said. "Bayleef and I will win next time!"

Ash looked at the Park Ball in his hand. He knew what he wanted to do.

"Here," he said, handing the Park Ball to Casey. "Will you raise this Beedrill for me?"

"You mean it?" Casey said.

Ash nodded. "You really helped me out today."

"Thanks, Ash," Casey said. "I'll raise this Beedrill well. You can count on me!"

As he and Casey said good-bye, Brock and Misty caught up to them.

"Congratulations, Ash," Misty said.

"I told you I was on a winning streak," Ash said.

"You may be right," Misty said. "I hope you can keep it up!"

9

The Pokémon Dojo

Ash wanted to hurry to the next gym in Ecruteak City.

"I can't wait to earn my next gym badge," he said. "At the rate I'm going, I can't lose!"

The friends were walking through a mountain pass. The dirt trail wound down the mountain and tall trees rose up on either side of them.

Suddenly, a panicked voice rang through the crisp mountain air.

"Help! Somebody stop it!"

Ash spun around to see a large Tauros

thundering toward them on the trail. The Wild Bull Pokémon had two sharp horns on its head and three tails. A man was running behind it, trying to catch it. Ash guessed it must be the Tauros's trainer.

"Whoa!" Ash said. He, Brock, Misty, and Pikachu leaped out of the way just in time.

The Tauros ran past them down the hill. Further down, Ash could see an old man walking with his back to the Tauros. He hadn't heard the warning cry.

"That old man's in trouble!" Ash cried. Without hesitation, he cut through the trees, hoping to get to the man before Tauros did.

"Run for it, sir!" he yelled.

Ash threw a Poké Ball in the air, and Bulbasaur burst out in a blaze of light. The small Pokémon had a plant bulb on its sturdy back.

The old man turned around. He eyed the charging Tauros. He started to move, but then saw Ash's Bulbasaur.

"What are you going to do with that Bulbasaur?" he asked Ash.

"Bulbasaur, use Vine Whip to stop Tauros," Ash called out.

Bulbasaur stepped out onto the trail between the old man and Tauros. Green vines lashed out of Bulbasaur's plant bulb. The vines wrapped around Tauros's horns.

Tauros roared and charged toward Bulbasaur.

"Dodge it, Bulbasaur!" Ash called out.

The Grass Pokémon jumped out of the way at the last second. Tauros spun around, angry, and headed toward Bulbasaur again.

"Now aim Vine Whip at Tauros's feet," Ash said.

More vines flew out of Bulbasaur's back. The vines wrapped around Tauros's feet. The Pokémon couldn't move.

"Finish it up with Sleep Powder!" Ash shouted.

Glimmering powder floated out of the plant bulb and covered Tauros. The Poké-

mon's eyes drooped, and seconds later it crashed to the ground, deep in sleep.

Just then, the Tauros's trainer ran up, panting and out of breath.

"Thanks for helping me," he said. "A Beedrill stung my Tauros, and it really flipped out."

The trainer held out a Poké Ball, and Tauros disappeared inside.

The old man held out his hand. "My name is Kenzo," he said. "I admire the way you have raised your Bulbasaur. Would you like to come over to my house for a little while?"

"Sure," Ash said. He could always use a break from the trail. Besides, with his long, white mustache and gray robe, Kenzo seemed like an interesting person.

Kenzo led them down the trail to a large wooden ranch house. In a courtyard in front of the house, several young Pokémon trainers were working out with their Pokémon.

As they got closer, Ash noticed they were all Fighting Pokémon. There was Mankey,

58

and Primeape, the evolved form of Mankey. A boy worked with a small blue Machop.

"I run a dojo," Kenzo explained. "It's a training center for Fighting Pokémon."

Ash nodded. Then he noticed that one girl was working with a Pokémon he had never seen before. The girl had pink hair and wore a white shirt, shorts, and boots. Her Pokémon came up to the top of her shoulder. It had two ball-shaped hands, short legs, and a round tail. But the coolest thing about it was the point on top of its head.

"One, two, one, two," chanted the girl. The Pokémon jumped upside down and spun around on the point.

Ash took out Dexter to find out more about it.

"Hitmontop, the Handstand Pokémon," the Pokédex said. "Don't be distracted by their smooth, dance-like kicks or you'll feel the power behind these attacks."

Ash and the others watched as the Hitmontop gracefully spun around the court-yard.

"That's a pretty cool dance," Misty said.

"Hmmph," said Kenzo. "Martial arts aren't meant for performance."

Soon the trainers stopped their workouts. One by one, they bowed to Kenzo and left the courtyard. The only one to remain was the girl with the Hitmontop.

"Why is everyone bowing to you?" Ash asked.

"I am the Shihan of this dojo," Kenzo replied.

"Shihan? Is that some sort of new Poké-mon?" Ash asked.

Kenzo's face turned bright red. Brock quickly jumped in.

"The Shihan is the strongest member of a dojo," he explained.

The pink-haired girl approached them. "Who are these people, Grandfather?" she asked.

Kenzo put an arm around Ash. "I have finally found someone to take my place," he said.

The girl looked shocked. Ash couldn't believe what he had heard.

"Take your place? You mean, me?" he asked.

"But, Grandfather, what about me?" asked the girl.

Kenzo shook his head. "You can't take over this dojo, Chigusa," he said. "All your Pokémon do is dance. The leader of this dojo must understand true fighting technique."

Chigusa turned to Ash, an angry look on

her face. "Fine, then," she said. "If you want to take over this dojo, you'll have to face me in a Pokémon battle first."

Ash tried to explain. "But I don't know anything about this. I don't want to —"

"I'll take you on!"

Ash and Chigusa turned at the sound of a deep voice. A tall man in black pants and a red shirt stood at the entrance to the courtyard. His long blue hair was tied back in a ponytail.

"I have come to challenge the Shihan of this dojo!" said the mysterious stranger.

10

Hitmontop vs. Hitmonlee

"My name is Shiro," said the man. "I am a warrior in training."

Kenzo's eyes narrowed. "Shiro, eh? Then you are the Dojo Destroyer who has been wreaking havoc in fighting dojos all over this area."

"None other," said Shiro. "I have defeated nine dojo leaders. You will be the tenth."

"We'll see about that," Kenzo said. "Our dojo won't fall so easily."

Chigusa was chosen to judge the battle. Ash watched, fascinated, from the sidelines.

Kenzo and Shiro were experts on Fighting Pokémon. This battle was sure to be exciting.

Kenzo and Shiro faced each other from across the battlefield. Shiro threw the first Poké Ball.

"Go, Hitmonlee!" he cried.

A strange-looking Pokémon burst from the ball. Hitmonlee had a bullet-shaped body. Each of its hands had three fingers. Its powerful legs were strong and sturdy. Hitmonlee had two large eyes but no nose or mouth.

"Hitmonlee, the kicking Pokémon," said Dexter. "This nimble Pokémon is able to launch a string of kicks from any position."

"A worthy opponent," said Kenzo, but he didn't seem worried. "Come out, Machoke."

Kenzo hurled the Poké Ball with all his might. A look of pain spread across his face as his back twisted like a pretzel.

Kenzo's throw affected Machoke, too. The muscled gray Pokémon cringed and grabbed its back.

"Grandfather! You've strained your back," Chigusa said, running over to him.

Kenzo gritted his teeth and nodded.

"Don't worry," Chigusa said. "I'll take over this battle."

"Ridiculous," Kenzo said. "You can't win." He tried to stand up straight, but fell over.

"We have no choice," Chigusa said. "We must defend the honor of this dojo."

Shiro shrugged. "I don't care who I fight," he said.

Brock took Chigusa's place as judge. Chigusa faced Shiro and Hitmonlce with Hitmontop by her side.

"Begin!" Brock shouted.

"Hitmonlee! Rolling Kick!" Shiro shouted his command.

Hitmonlee jumped up and extended its right leg. It aimed the kick at Hitmontop's head, but the smaller Pokémon held up its hand to block the kick.

"Show it how a proper Rolling Kick looks," Chigusa told Hitmontop.

Hitmontop delivered a quick kick to Hitmonlee's side.

"Keep up that rhythm," Chigusa said.

Wham! Wham! Wham! Hitmontop delivered a kick with its left foot, then its right foot, then left again. It pummeled Hitmonlee with an almost musical rhythm.

"All right, Hitmontop. Rapid Spin!" Chigusa called out.

Hitmontop flipped upside down and balanced on the point on its head. It spun around superfast, until its legs and round feet were a blur.

Hitmontop spun faster and faster, aiming right at Hitmonlee. Ash knew that if Hit-

montop made contact, Hitmonlee would be knocked to the ground.

"It's coming, Hitmonlee," Shiro warned.

Hitmonlee responded with a powerful kick to Hitmontop's spinning feet. The move stopped Hitmontop in its tracks. The Pokémon toppled to the ground.

Bam! Hitmonlee continued the attack with a strong punch, knocking Hitmontop backward.

"Hitmonlee, High Jump Kick!" yelled Shiro.

Hitmonlee jumped up and delivered a punishing kick to Hitmontop. It was too much for the smaller Pokémon. It lay sprawled on the ground — and it didn't look like it could get up. Ash looked at Chigusa. She wore a devastated look on her face.

"Let's end this, Hitmonlee," Shiro said.

Suddenly, a cloud of black smoke exploded on the battlefield. Ash's eyes burned.

When the smoke cleared, Ash made out the Team Rocket balloon in the sky above. But that wasn't all.

A net dangled from the balloon basket. And trapped in the net were Hitmonlee and Hitmontop!

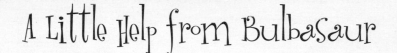

11

A Little Help from Bulbasaur

"These Fighting Pokémon don't stand a *fighting* chance against us." Jessie chuckled. She began to pull up the net. "We'll be leaving now with your Hitmontop and Hitmonlee."

"No you won't," Ash said. "Bulbasaur, Razor Leaf!"

Sharp green leaves flew from the plant bulb on Bulbasaur's back. They severed the top of the net, sending the Fighting Pokémon tumbling safely to the ground.

Jessie and James scowled angrily.

"Go, Arbok!" Jessie shouted as the purple Pokémon slithered from its Poké Ball.

"Go, Victreebel!" yelled James. A tall Pokémon that looked like a yellow flower bell exploded onto the scene. Victreebel promptly swallowed James in its big mouth.

"Hey, quit that!" James complained.

While James tried to free himself from his Pokémon, Jessie began her attack. She ordered Arbok to use Poison Sting.

Sharp little darts flew from Arbok's mouth. Ash knew that if the darts made contact, the fighting Pokémon would be knocked out by their poison.

Luckily, Hitmonlee and Hitmontop jumped out of the way just in time.

"Victreebel, Sleep Powder!" James called out.

Victreebel jumped down from the balloon basket. Shining powder poured from its mouth. The powder hit Hitmonlee right in the face. Shiro's Pokémon toppled backward and began snoring.

"Pikachu!" Ash yelled.

Pikachu jumped up and slammed into Victreebel, sending the bigger Pokémon flying back into the balloon basket.

That took care of Victreebel. Ash called on Bulbasaur next.

"You handle Arbok, Bulbasaur," Ash told his Pokémon.

Bulbasaur shot its plant vines and wrapped them around Arbok's body. It swung Arbok around and around, sending it flying into the balloon.

"Now, use Razor Leaf!" Ash cried.

Bulbasaur launched several sharp leaves at the hot-air balloon. They tore the thin fabric. Team Rocket careened off into the distance as air shot out of the holes.

"Looks like Team Rocket's blasting off again!" they wailed.

Shiro looked a little shaken up. "We were interrupted," he said. "Let's finish the match tomorrow."

Chigusa agreed. Kenzo led them all inside the dojo, where he fixed a light supper.

"I won't lose tomorrow," Chigusa promised her grandfather.

Kenzo shook his head. "You never learn," he said. He turned to Ash. "Would you use your Bulbasaur to teach my grandchild a few things?"

Ash couldn't believe a dojo master was asking for his help. "I'm not sure if I'm qualified," he said.

"I think it will be good for Chigusa," Kenzo said.

"Fine," said Chigusa sharply. She rose from the table. "Let's see what you have to teach me."

Ash had only had a few bites of food, but he couldn't resist the tone of challenge in Chigusa's voice.

"We'll do this training as though it were a battle," Kenzo said, when they were back outside on the battle area. "Begin!"

Ash started by asking Bulbasaur to put a spin on its Vine Whip. The green vine spun around in a circle, like a lasso.

"Imagine that this Vine Whip is Hitmonlee's Kick Attack," he told Chigusa.

"I see," Chigusa said. "This might be decent training after all."

Chigusa countered by asking Hitmontop to do a Rolling Kick. Hitmontop spun around on the point on its head. At the same time, it aimed kicks at Bulbasaur with its feet.

Bulbasaur expertly dodged each kick. Then it launched a vine at the point on Hitmontop's head.

Hitmontop lost its balance and crashed to the ground. The Fighting Pokémon jumped back to its feet.

"Use Vine Whip on Hitmontop's head and legs," Ash said.

Bulbasaur used its vines the way Hitmonlee would use its strong legs. It hit Hitmontop in the head and legs, causing it to fall again.

"Tackle!" Ash yelled.

Before Hitmontop could get up, Bulbasaur slammed into it. Hitmontop went flying.

This time it couldn't get up.

"Chigusa loses," said Kenzo. "Ash's side was stronger."

"Not by much," Chigusa said stubbornly.

"Hitmontop's spin is what did you in," Kenzo said. "It's a strong attack because it confuses your opponent. But it also makes it hard for Hitmontop to read the next attack. As Hitmontop's trainer, you should be watching your opponent and guiding your Pokémon."

"You mean I didn't cover well enough," Chigusa said.

Kenzo nodded. "You are too busy trying to keep the rhythm. Your attacks look pretty, but you must work *with* your Pokémon to win in battle."

"When it comes to working closely with Pokémon, Ash is as good as anyone," Brock remarked.

"You're right there," Misty agreed. Even Togepi chirped up.

Chigusa nodded. "I finally get it," she said. "All right, Ash. Can you teach me how to become a winner?"

Ash grinned. "You're asking the right person!"

Ash and Chigusa trained all night. Although he felt tired, Ash didn't stop. This was too important.

He had to help Chigusa. If she lost the battle against Shiro tomorrow, the dojo would lose. And Ash would lose, too. It would mean he had failed as a teacher.

When the sun rose over the hills the next morning, Ash and Chigusa were still working. Brock, Misty, Pikachu, and Togepi had fallen asleep on the soft grass.

Shiro didn't waste any time. He appeared back at the dojo as soon as it was morning.

"Let's finish this battle," he said.

12

Working Together

"Begin!" Brock yelled.

"Hitmonlee, go!" Shiro shouted.

Hitmonlee charged toward Hitmontop. Chigusa ordered Hitmontop to perform Rapid Spin. Her Pokémon twirled across the field like a mini-tornado.

Shiro smiled smugly. "Hitmontop can't read our attacks while it is spinning. Hitmonlee, shower it with attacks!"

Chigusa ordered Hitmontop to jump back to its feet. The two Pokémon traded punches, but nothing connected. They were both moving too fast.

Hitmontop began spinning again. Shiro decided to counter with Rolling Kicks from Hitmonlee.

Hitmonlee aimed kick after kick at Hitmontop. But Chigusa kept her eyes on her opponent. She yelled out directions to Hitmontop.

"Left! Now right! Now left!"

By listening to Chigusa, Hitmontop was able to dodge each kick and keep spinning.

"It worked!" Ash cried. He could see that Shiro looked shaken.

"Your defenses have gotten better," Shiro said. "Hitmonlee, take out its balance with Double Kick!"

"The kicks are coming from straight ahead," Chigusa warned Hitmontop.

Hitmonlee aimed two quick kicks at Hitmontop, but Hitmontop leaned in and blocked the kicks with its feet.

"Hitmontop, upright Rapid Spin!" Chigusa shouted.

Ash held his breath. He knew from their practice the night before that this was a tricky move. Could Hitmontop pull it off?

Hitmontop jumped up and began spinning sideways on its feet, almost like a windmill. The sideways attacks were faster and more powerful than when Hitmontop was upside down.

Shiro's eyes widened. He clearly had not seen anything like this before.

"Hitmonlee, go directly into Triple Kick!"

Hitmonlee tried to deliver a powerful kick, but Hitmontop was just too fast for it.

"Hitmontop, spin in midair!" Chigusa called out.

Hitmontop gathered up speed, then launched itself high into the air. It came speeding to the ground like a fallen rocket.

Hitmonlee couldn't escape. Hitmontop was just too fast.

Slam! Hitmontop knocked into Shiro's Pokémon.

Hitmonlee crashed to the ground.

Ash waited. Would Hitmonlee get up?

The answer was no. Hitmonlee was down and out.

"Hitmonlee is incapable of battle," Brock announced. "Hitmontop wins!"

"We did it!" Chigusa cheered. She ran out to the field and hugged Hitmontop.

"That was an excellent strategy," Shiro admitted. "You fought a good battle."

"I'm going to study with my grandfather to become an even better trainer," Chigusa

said. She turned to Ash. "Thanks for your help."

"No problem," Ash said. "I'm just glad you won."

"Let me guess," Misty said. "Your winning streak is still intact, right?"

"It feels good to help someone else win," Ash said. "But I'm not done winning myself."

"I don't know, Ash," Brock said. "I think you're already a winner." He pointed to Pikachu and Bulbasaur.

Ash hugged his Pokémon.

"That's right," Ash said. "As long as I've got my Pokémon, I can't lose!"

About the Author

Tracey West has been writing books for more than ten years. When she's not playing the blue version of the Pokémon game (she started with a Squirtle), she enjoys reading comic books, watching cartoons, and taking long walks in the woods (looking for wild Pokémon). She lives in a small town in New York with her family and pets.

POKéMON

GOTTA READ 'EM ALL!™